The Day Jean-Pierre Joined The Circus

PAUL GALLICO

THE DAY JEAN-PIERRE
JOINED THE CIRCUS

Illustrated by
GIOIA FIAMMENGHI

HEINEMANN : LONDON

To
BRIGID THERESA
YOUNG

William Heinemann Ltd
LONDON MELBOURNE TORONTO
JOHANNESBURG AUCKLAND

Printed and bound in Great Britain by
Bookprint Limited, Crawley, Sussex

CHAPTER I

THE AFFAIR which was to result in such a change in the lives of Cecile Durand and her Guinea Pig Jean-Pierre, began on a quiet, autumn Sunday afternoon. It was not at all the time that one would expect anything to happen.

The Durands lived on a flower farm in the hills behind Cannes, in the South of France. There, Monsieur Durand, Cecile's father, raised all the lovely blooms for which that part of the world is famous.

But on Sunday no one worked. Everyone did as he or she pleased to enjoy the day of rest. Cecile was amusing herself with Jean-Pierre, going through the keepsakes that had marked his adventures ever since they had been together.

She was eleven, a dark-haired girl with round, serious eyes and a pleasant face. She had many animal friends: the dog named Bobi, Coco the cat and Gris-Gris, a rabbit. But her special pet was the long-haired, Abyssinian Guinea Pig; she dearly loved this funny little creature, who was not even very beautiful. He looked something like a cross between a clothes brush and a feather duster; his browny-black fur was rough and sometimes tangled. But he had proud white whiskers, a most delectable pink nose, pink feet and golden eyes.

That afternoon Cecile and Jean-Pierre were surrounded by souvenirs of his fabulous experiences, which she had laid out on the floor.

There was the receipt from the pet shop: 'Sold to Mademoiselle Cecile Durand, one Guinea Pig. Five Francs', proof that Jean-Pierre belonged to her alone. Next to it was the blue ribbon he had won at a children's pet show. Then there was a copy of the poster that the police had issued at the time Jean-Pierre had been pignapped. It showed a photograph of him and the legend in large letters: 'LOST, STRAYED OR STOLEN. REWARD'.

There were the thrilling letters with foreign stamps from far-away places, which had been written to Cecile by kindly people who had encountered Jean-Pierre on his famous trip-around-the-world mix-up.

'And here you are in Australia with Mr Flippo the Clown, and inside Angelique,' said Cecile to Jean-Pierre, and pointed out two photographs.

One was of a chalk-faced comic with two crosses for eyes, a big red bulb of a nose, a huge red mouth painted in the shape of an eternal smile, and he was holding Jean-Pierre. The other was of a kangaroo wearing a conical hat and, peering out of her pouch with a miniature headgear of the same kind, was none other than Jean-Pierre himself.

As she looked at these, Cecile thought of the halfway-around-the-world telephone call from Mr Flippo. She seemed to hear once more his special, put-on, funny laughter, 'Tee-hee-hee-hee-hee-heeeeee!'.

All this had happened over a year ago, but Cecile had never forgotten the thrill of speaking to the clown and hearing Jean-Pierre clicking his teeth and sneezing, which he did when he was excited, over the telephone from far-off Sydney, Australia.

'It's all because you're magic, Jean-Pierre,' Cecile said.

Or, at least he had been slightly so in the past, in the days when she and Jean-Pierre had talked to one another. But Cecile had been eight years old then. Now that she was eleven, going on twelve, really magic things did not come about so often. But this neither surprised nor worried her, for she was growing up.

When one is very young, the world is full of magic, but as one grows older and has a great deal more work to do and school becomes more difficult, there is not so much time to notice.

3

Down through the years, Cecile's love for Jean-Pierre had increased if anything, and the things that had happened to him made him all the more precious. Now she picked him up and held him high in the air, looking into his golden eyes, and crying, 'Oh, Jean-Pierre, you're wonderful! Never, never, never leave me. I love you!'

At that moment, from without came the most astonishing series of bangings, clatterings, clankings, wheezings, coughs and explosions, coupled with the sound of tyres on the gravel driveway leading to the farm.

'My goodness, Jean-Pierre, what do you suppose that could be?'

'Hello!' said Monsieur Durand in the living-room below, laying down his paper. 'Who on earth can that be, and whatever do they want?' For the late Sunday afternoon was not a calling time. He got up to have a look.

'Well, I must say!' remarked Madame Durand in the kitchen. She was putting the finishing touches to an apricot tart to be baked for their supper, and peered out from behind the curtain.

A car had drawn up in front of the house. Both it and its driver were ancient and shabby. The machine, dusty and dented, still held together but it looked as though it were not going to do so much longer. Perhaps the very next trip it would collapse into many pieces.

The man who sat at the wheel looked the same. He wore an old-fashioned grey suit, and a slightly too-small, grey hat sat on the top of his head. His eyes were sad and curiously turned down at the corners. His mouth, too, drooped and the grey skin on which there was a faint white stubble, sagged beneath his chin. Only his long nose seemed droll.

As the three Durands watched, the stranger got out of his car. He was tall, thin and seemed to be very old, and if anything resembled a scarecrow. For his suit hung loosely about him. The sleeves were too short, the trousers baggy and the shoes scuffed.

He gazed about him in a rather vague and helpless manner, as though he did not know exactly where he was.

'Hmmmm,' muttered Monsieur Durand, 'the sooner we get rid of that one, the better.'

'Oh, the poor man!' said Madame Durand. 'He looks as though he were lost—and so tired. Perhaps he would like a drop of something.'

And Cecile up in her bedroom? Ordinarily she would not have had any interest in the arrival of an adult at the farm. For it was always someone who had business with her father about seeds, or plants, or fertilizers, or a new species of rose. But such an odd-appearing stranger on a Sunday afternoon was something else again. Her curiosity was aroused. Yet she did not have the slightest suspicion of how greatly this was to concern her.

'You wait here,' she said to Jean-Pierre, and put him on the floor close to the photographs of the clown and the kangaroo. 'I'll just go and find out who it is and come right back.'

And so it was that all three of the Durands emerged from the door practically at the same time. As they did so, the man raised the too-small hat a few inches from his grey hair and said politely, 'Have I the pleasure of addressing the family Durand?'

'Yes,' replied Cecile's father. 'My name is André Durand. What is it you wish?'

'Only to have a few words with you, if you'll forgive the intrusion. For I have driven a long way to see you. My name is Marcel Pasquini.'

He seemed so weary and dispirited that he at once touched the heart of Madame Durand. She said, 'But of course! You must come in, and perhaps take something to refresh you.'

Monsieur Pasquini replaced the too-small hat upon his head, gave Cecile a long and searching look, and then smiled at her. And when he smiled, all the sadness wrinkles went out of his grey face and turned most curiously to laughter crinkles.

Cecile smiled back at him. She could not help herself. It was almost as though his face were made of rubber, the manner in which it had so quickly changed when he had gazed at her, and she wondered why. She also thought what a strange name— Pasquini. It sounded Italian. Whatever he had come for, this did not seem to be going to have anything to do with flowers or fertilizers.

Monsieur Durand opened the door. Madame Durand entered, but when her husband motioned to Monsieur Pasquini to follow, he made a slight bow and indicated that Cecile was to go in front of him, which she did. And so they went in procession into the house.

And still Cecile had no inkling of who the visitor was or what he wanted.

CHAPTER II

THEY WENT into the beamed living room, where Madame Durand produced a bottle of *Pastis*. This is a strong liquid that tastes like aniseed and turns milky in water. She also brought a plate of biscuits and cheese. It was obvious that the man was hungry as well as tired, from the manner in which he fell upon the food, and after he had had a few sips of the drink, some colour began to come into his face and life into the sad eyes.

'Where have you come from?' enquired Madame Durand.

'From Tarbes.'

'Goodness, but that *is* a long way. Do have some more of the cheese.'

Monsieur Pasquini helped himself, and took a long draught of the *Pastis*. 'Yes, I left very early in the morning. And what is more, I shall have to be back there tonight—or rather, before tomorrow.'

'And you have come all that way just to see us?' exclaimed Madame Durand, now thoroughly astonished. For she had never laid eyes upon the man before and she was certain neither had her husband.

Monsieur Pasquini wiped his lips with the napkin on the tray and gave a sigh, which was now more one of contentment than fatigue. He no longer looked quite so old and downcast. 'Yes,' he repeated, 'all that way, just to see you,' and once more it was upon Cecile that his glance rested. But none of the Durands noticed this.

'Well,' said Monsieur Durand, 'I can only say that without having the honour of knowing you, I am greatly flattered that you should have come such a distance.'

Monsieur Pasquini did not reply but only bowed his head. There was something rather stately in the way he did it.

Monsieur Durand broke the silence that followed with, 'If, then, you feel sufficiently refreshed to wish to state your business with me—if it is private, we can go into my office. . . .'

'Oh, no, no, no, nothing private. . . .' The visitor hesitated and then continued, 'As a matter of fact, my business is not with you at all, but rather with that young lady there, who I take it is Cecile. . . .'

Cecile, who did not find the occasion entertaining, had been just about to say, 'Please may I be excused?', but now she swallowed the words and stared at the stranger. Business with *her*? And how did he come to know her name, since neither her father nor mother had mentioned it?

'What?' It was the turn of Monsieur Durand to cry out in astonishment. 'You have driven all that way from Tarbes to see my daughter? You know Cecile?'

'Yes,' replied the old man gravely, 'I know her.' And then turning to Cecile he asked, 'And do you not know me?'

Bewildered, Cecile studied Monsieur Pasquini. She was certain she had never met him. Silently she shook her head.

'Well, that is not too surprising,' he smiled, and they all noticed at the same time how sweet his smile could be, 'since neither of us has ever seen the other before. Still. . . .' And here he suddenly threw back his head and laughed a curiously shrill and affected kind of laugh: 'Tee-hee-hee-hee-hee-heeeee, tee-hee-hee-hee-heeeee!'

Something very like a trickle of iced water seemed to run down Cecile's spine. The man was a stranger to her indeed, but when and where had she heard that laugh? Why, it seemed to have been in her ears only a short while ago. It was so very familiar, as though once heard never forgotten.

'Tee-hee-hee-hee-heeee,' he nickered again.

And then Cecile KNEW! Sydney, Australia! The telephone call during Jean-Pierre's trip around the world. 'Oh!' she cried, 'You're Mr Flippo, the clown!'

Monsieur Pasquini arose, did another of his grave and dignified bows and said, 'Yes, I am Mr Flippo. That is my stage name.'

Cecile gave another cry, 'Oh! Dear Mr Flippo!' ran over to him, threw her arms about his neck and kissed him on the cheek. 'Thank you, thank you, for being so kind to Jean-Pierre. How could I know you when the picture you sent me was in your funny costume? I was just looking at it again, upstairs.'

Smiling, he held her off from him and said, 'You're exactly as I imagined you would be from your voice and from what Jean-Pierre told me about you.'

'Oh, Jean-Pierre!' exclaimed Cecile. 'How happy he will be to see you! May I go and fetch him, Monsieur . . . Monsieur. . . . How is it you wish to be called?'

'Flippo,' said the circus clown, 'just plain old Flippo. That's what everybody calls me.' And now a further transformation seemed to take place in him, which had begun with Cecile's mention of Jean-Pierre. More of the years, the slouch, the sag and the sadness seemed to fall away from him. He looked straighter and younger as she ran from the room.

In a moment she was back with the Guinea Pig in her cupped hands. 'Look, Jean-Pierre, it's your old friend Mr Flippo. Here, take him!'

'Well, well!' said Mr Flippo, and held him to his cheek. 'Whoever would have thought that you and I would meet again?'

Jean-Pierre sniffed and snuffled and then sneezed four times. He then made little clicking noises and appeared to be quite happy where he was.

'He knows you! He remembers you, too,' cried Cecile, enchanted. What a wonderful and surprising Sunday this had suddenly turned out to be.

There was no way of telling really whether Jean-Pierre did recognize Mr Flippo, particularly since he was not wearing his clown make-up. But one thing was certain: he was content to be held by him.

Well, and then suddenly they were all friends and relaxed as though they had known one another all their lives. Mr Flippo told the story from his end of what had happened that night in Sydney.

'Our circus was pitched next to the airport. I was sitting in my tent, making up my face for the evening performance when a fellow, all blue uniform and gold braid, came in carrying a travelling box with a Guinea Pig inside it and a note indicating that its name was Jean-Pierre and that it belonged to Cecile Durand. She had left instructions for care and feeding in case something should go wrong. Well, it was obvious that something had gone very wrong indeed.

' "There's not another plane out until late tomorrow", the freight agent said, "and if anything happens to the beast, they'll have our heads off. Somebody remembered that you had some trained pigs and other animals and would know how to look after it properly. If you will agree, we will pick it up before flight time. You'll be doing us a great favour. We'll even pay for a telephone

call to the child in Paris, so you can tell her that her pet is all right."

'And so there we were,' continued Mr Flippo, cuddling Jean-Pierre in his lap. 'I thought he might be lonely after all that time in his cage and so I took him and introduced him to Angelique, my trained kangaroo. Oh, but she's clever! And I've taught her to do more tricks than a monkey. But just at that time she was sad and hardly wished to work in the ring with me, for she had had a baby and it died. On an impulse I put Jean-Pierre into her pouch. Well, you never would believe the difference, eh, old boy?' And here he held Jean-Pierre up in his two hands and looked into his yellow-gold eyes. Jean-Pierre sneezed enthusiastically three times.

'From then on Angelique was a different woman—or, a kangaroo, I should say, and wouldn't let me take Jean-Pierre away from her.'

He lowered Jean-Pierre once more. 'All this happened around seven o'clock in the evening and the performance was scheduled for half-past-eight. What was there to do but to let Angelique take Jean-Pierre into the ring with her? I made a little hat for him, like

the one Angelique wore in her act, and when he peered out of her pouch, I can tell you it was a sensation. People laughed and screamed and clapped and cheered. And here . . .' Mr Flippo turned Jean-Pierre around so that he was facing the Durands.

'And here you have him. Behold the only Guinea Pig to become a star overnight. For the next day his picture was in all the papers.'

Cecile clapped her hands with pleasure, took Jean-Pierre from Mr Flippo and held him to her. She considered herself really the luckiest girl in the world to have such a pet.

'And now your circus has come to France?' asked Monsieur Durand.

'No,' replied Mr Flippo, 'it's quite a different one. It's very small. I no longer have my pigs. There's only Angelique and me left. It's called the *Cirque Frenet*. We have come up through Spain and are playing in Tarbes tomorrow, which is why I must be back.'

He paused for a moment. Some of the brightness and excitement that had illuminated him for a little seemed to go out of him.

'From Tarbes we shall be moving northwards and so this was the only time I could expect to be far enough south for a call upon you.'

It was Madame Durand who said, 'What a splendid person you must be, Monsieur Pasquini, to expose yourself to two such exhausting and tedious drives just to give pleasure to a little girl you have never even met, except on the telephone.'

But at this, instead of being pleased, Mr Flippo seemed to sag even more and he appeared what he was—a weary, lonely, and worried old man.

He did not even look at them, his sad eyes were turned to the floor as he said huskily and in a voice that they could hardly hear, 'Madame, you are too kind and above all, too trusting. I am afraid there is another motive for my visit.'

The sudden change of his attitude now affected them all and particularly Cecile, who found herself quite suddenly feeling ill at ease and a little frightened. They were all silent, waiting for him to go on.

He shuffled his feet miserably for a moment and then, still without looking up, mumbled, 'I came to ask whether Mademoiselle here, Cecile, would not perhaps agree to sell me Jean-Pierre?'

CHAPTER III

'SELL JEAN-PIERRE!' cried Cecile in horror, hardly able to believe her ears. 'Oh, I would never do that!'

'Sell Jean-Pierre!' echoed her mother, taken completely by surprise by the oddness of the request.

'Is that what you came all the way here for?' queried Monsieur Durand, likewise amazed.

Mr Flippo appeared to shrink further inside his clothes and with his sad, droopy eyes and sagging jowls looked like a mournful bloodhound, one who had just been beaten.

15

He glanced from one to the other, his gaze resting for a moment on the small Guinea Pig which Cecile was now holding close to her breast, as though she were afraid he might be snatched away from her suddenly. Then he said, 'Forgive me. I was a fool even to dream of such a possibility. You have been most kind to receive me and I have imposed upon your hospitality. Thank you for the refreshments and now I will go.' And he rose from his chair.

But Monsieur Durand stopped the old man with a motion of his hand and said, 'Wait! Won't you tell us why you wish to buy my daughter's pet?'

'Because,' said Mr Flippo, 'I need him desperately.'

He had not meant to say that, nor with such distress. But it was a cry of despair torn from his heart. When he realized what he had done, he stood unhappily in the middle of the room, making vague and helpless gestures with his hands and mumbling, 'I didn't mean that. I must be going.'

'No!' said Monsieur Durand authoritatively, but kindly, 'Not yet. Won't you sit down and tell us about it? You are in trouble . . .'

Some starch began to return to the figure of Mr Flippo, and he said, 'Well, if you insist.'

'But we do insist,' put in Madame Durand. 'You who have been so kind to our daughter. Come, let me pour you another small *Pastis* and perhaps it will make it easier for you.'

And so Mr Flippo, after one or two swallows of the milky liquid, sat on the edge of his chair, twirling his hat in his hands and began. It was the story of his gradual decline from one of the featured clowns in a large and prosperous circus, to a fallen-by-the-wayside old man, whose act was no longer wanted and who was about to be turned out.

An epidemic of swine fever in Melbourne had killed off his valuable trained pigs. A further disaster of a fire in the animal quarters had cost the lives of two of his kangaroos. He had only just managed to save Angelique. After this the circus had failed

'Angelique and I worked our way back to Europe,' he told them. 'But you know, times are changing and children and audiences, too. There are not many circuses now, and most people would rather sit at home and look at the telly than go to the show.

'I was taken on by Frenet's. But business was poor and a single, trained animal act is not much of an attraction. Michel Frenet is not a bad fellow, but he has himself to look after. He would have been willing to give me another chance if . . .'

Mr Flippo did not finish this sentence and the 'if' seemed to hang there in the room, quivering in the air for a moment. Without knowing that she was doing so, Cecile squeezed Jean-Pierre to her so tightly that he squeaked.

'Yes, go on,' encouraged Monsieur Durand, 'if . . . ?'

Mr Flippo's smile was now resigned and he merely replied, 'It's the "if", which I realize now, is of course impossible.'

'Yet you still owe us the rest of the story, I think,' suggested Monsieur Durand.

'Well,' Mr Flippo began reluctantly, but later warmed to his tale, 'yesterday morning Frenet came to the clown tent to give me my notice. I knew he was going to do so and was already beginning to arrange things in my trunk, sorting out all my old scrapbooks and notices from the newspapers. And I can tell you that my animals and I made many headlines.

'As I told you,' Mr Flippo went on, 'he isn't a bad fellow. He was sympathetic and clapped me on the back saying, "It's too bad, Flippo, but you know how it is. If you could only work out something brand new or brilliant with your animal, which would be a draw to the crowds, we'd give you another chance."

'Then, looking over my shoulder,' continued the clown, 'Frenet pointed and said, "Hello, what's that?" He was glancing at the picture on page one of the *Sydney Morning Herald*, of myself, Angelique wearing her clown hat and peering out of her pouch, with his own little hat, Jean-Pierre.

' "Now that's something like it," he said and rapped the news-paper with his knuckles. "Why, that's marvellously funny and I'm sure would be a tremendous attraction. What's that little animal? A Guinea Pig? Well, get yourself one and we'll renew your contract then and there. Why, just that picture on the posters alone will be enough to pull them in." '

'*Eh bien*,' said Monsieur Durand. 'Why didn't you, then? It couldn't be so difficult to come by a Guinea Pig.'

Flippo's voice suddenly sounded harsh as he cried, 'And don't you think I've tried? Do you take me for a fool? I, who have been in show business for fifty years! Why, with the success and excite-ment created by that single appearance of Angelique with her

Guinea Pig in her pouch, we would have become stars at five
times our salary. The very same day, back in Australia, only a few
hours after Jean-Pierre's departure, I had already purchased
several of them.'

His very vehemence and the fires that had suddenly lit up his
dull eyes held his audience spellbound and hanging on every word.

'And then what happened?' queried Monsieur Durand.

The fires went out and Flippo collapsed back into the chair.
'Angelique!' he said. 'She would have none of them. I tried every
kind, size, shape and colour. I imported Abyssinian, Peruvian and
Canadian Guinea Pigs. I tried male and female: black, brown,
white, mixed, mottled. I even advertised for those who had been
pets, always hoping to find another that Angelique would accept.
As fast as I put one into her pouch, she popped it out again. I then
realized that it was Jean-Pierre, and Jean-Pierre alone, that she
had loved and hence permitted him to remain where once her own
baby had lived. It was Jean-Pierre or nothing, and so I gave up
and forgot about it.'

The strangeness of this dilemma struck home to all three and not even Monsieur Durand had anything further to say.

'You can imagine, then, my feelings when Michel Frenet tapped that old newspaper and offered me a chance if I could make it a part of my act. Suddenly the thought struck me: *I'm in France—in the same country as Jean-Pierre.* Soon we would be moving north. Here was my one chance. It struck me perhaps that Mademoiselle Cecile—a year or so older—might have outgrown her pet somewhat and perhaps could be persuaded to sell him to me and to Angelique. Well, there now, you have had all of the thoughts of a silly old man who has only managed to cause you a great deal of trouble and inconvenience.'

Yet he did not make any move to go but sat slumped in his chair. Was it possible that he still nursed some idea that Cecile would part with her pet?

It was her father who felt that if there lingered any hope, it ought to be given its chance or quenched forever. And so he turned to his daughter and said to her, 'Well, Cecile, you have heard Monsieur Pasquini's story. What do you think?'

Cecile made no reply, for she was astonished to find anger growing inside her.

'It will have to be your decision,' continued Monsieur Durand. 'Jean-Pierre is yours, and only you can say what you will do.'

Cecile knew what her anger was about now. It was unfair of them, the grownups, to put such a responsibility upon her, to make her listen to a heartbreaking story from an old, unhappy man who had once done her pet a great kindness. It was unjust, wrong and wicked! Her fury burst its bounds. She stamped her foot and cried, 'No, no, no! I'll never sell him! I hate you! I hate you all!' And with that, hugging Jean-Pierre even more tightly to her breast, she ran from the room and out of the house.

CHAPTER IV

CECILE'S MOST secret and private place with Jean-Pierre was in the cellar. There she fed him his carrots, crumbs of bread, cake or cheese and pomegranate seeds, of which he was most fond. But she did not wish to go there as long as the horrid old man with the flabby, grey skin who was trying to take Jean-Pierre away from her, was in the house. And so she fled with her pet to the second most secret place, the glen where there was a grassy bank and a small stream shaded by a clump of olive trees. Here she threw herself down onto the grass and burst into tears.

Unfair, unfair, unfair! It was the first time that Cecile had come into contact with somebody else's trouble, or rather that somebody else had brought his problems and laid them at her feet. The experience was both novel and disturbing. For not only was it full of adult injustice, with which as a child she was not exactly unfamiliar, but also bursting with 'whys'.

Why would his silly old Angelique only let Jean-Pierre into her pouch? Why had there had to be swine fever to kill off all Flippo's marvellously trained pigs? Why were there less circuses than before? Why had just that page of the newspaper showing Jean-Pierre inside the kangaroo been turned up for the circus owner to see? In fact, as she dried her tears and thought about the story the old clown had told, there was a 'why' at every stop. And the biggest one of all was why did this have to happen to her, instead of to some other little girl?

But as she caressed and cuddled the Guinea Pig to comfort herself, an answer seemed at hand for the last one. It was because no other girl in the world had an Abyssinian Guinea Pig who was slightly magic and special.

In fact he was so special that a kangaroo named Angelique, whom he had met in Australia, would have no other Guinea Pig but him near her. And there she was right back again full circle to the sad, old man who had played such a sweet part in that great adventure and at whom she had just screamed that she hated him. She was not hating him any longer. She tried to continue doing so, but it would not work. She learned at that moment something of how difficult it is to keep a hate going. Cecile's anger turned to pity. She was genuinely sorry for Mr Flippo. Nevertheless she was not going to give up Jean-Pierre to him or to anyone else.

A green beetle with what looked like a fair pair of nippers at its front end, came out from under a leaf, tumbled off a stalk and advanced towards her, waving its feelers. When it had come to within a foot or so, its antennae told it, 'Hold it, chum! There seems to be a big obstacle there. Right-about-face!' It turned and ambled off in the direction of the brook that chuckled through the glen.

Cecile wondered what would have happened if the beetle had not decided to change its mind. It might have bitten her. Or, in a panic she could have squashed it. Or, she might have got up and run off. One way or another, whatever one did or did not do, always seemed to have some kind of an effect, good or bad.

What would happen if she let Mr Flippo have Jean-Pierre? And, what too, if she did not?

Well, Flippo had told them plainly enough what would be his fate. He would find himself stranded in some little town in France, with no job and a kangaroo to feed. He would surely go hungry himself before he let Angelique down, and he already looked too much skin and bones. But this was something she did not wish to think about. It made her feel all sad and once again responsible. To take her mind away she reflected upon life with a circus and what fun it must be.

They travelled to set up in a new town each day, to see new faces and new places. There would be those beautifully kept horses who were terribly clever and always knew in what order to trot around the ring, even when they were scrambled. One would be living with clowns and tightrope walkers, and jugglers. How marvellous it would be not only to know them, but to own and sleep in a gaily-painted wagon with a crooked chimney coming out of the roof.

And there would be the performance itself. Cecile had started

riding lessons when she was very young. Now she had an excellent seat upon a horse and was even becoming good at jumping. So of course in the circus she would be a bare-back rider in a spangled skirt. She saw herself turning handsprings as she ran clear across the ring, to fly up onto the back of a grey mare.

And, naturally, there would be no school, but instead gay costumes, music, coloured lights and excitement. And, above all, twice a day cheers and applause.

But that was the life that had been offered to Jean-Pierre. And he would become a star.

Now another thought followed swiftly. Supposing Mr Flippo had offered *her* the opportunity of joining up with him, and her parents, without an instant's reflection, had turned it down? How would she be feeling? And yet was not this exactly what she had done with Jean-Pierre?

And at this point Cecile experienced the most curious sinking in the pit of her stomach. It was the kind that often hits people when they realize that they might have been selfish and inconsiderate, and have suddenly caught a glimpse of the other side of the coin. Just because she had bought Jean-Pierre, did that give her the right to keep him from what might be a much more wonderful and attractive life for him? And if she loved him as much as she kept saying she did, perhaps she ought to be thinking of *him* more than of herself.

Not that Cecile was any little angel, or goody-goody. She did not like these thoughts that came to worry her. She tried to push them away and remember how angry she had been a little while before. But she was discovering that thoughts sometimes had a life of their own. They would not be brushed aside or blotted out, but kept jumping out from behind bushes or from under stones. They even floated upon the music of the little stream: *Jean-Pierre a star turn in the centre ring*; or *Jean-Pierre locked in a cage, waiting for her to come home from school? Mr Flippo in his clown makeup, bowing to thunders of applause*; or *old Monsieur Pasquini starving and broken-hearted*?

Which?

'Oh, Jean-Pierre, Jean-Pierre,' cried Cecile in despair, 'what *shall* I do?'

But the animal had no answer for her. He had crawled down from her lap. Busy and carefree, his fat little bottom turned towards her, he nipped off some kind of salad-like weed with two sharp front teeth. Sitting up and holding it daintily with his pink front paws, he ate it.

And then it happened. One moment Cecile could not think which way to turn and the next she knew. Clear as a bell the answer to her questions, or rather THE question, rang inside her.

And since this was the first time such a thing had occurred, it surprised her so that it seemed as though someone had spoken the words of her decision out loud: *There never really was any question, was there Cecile? There never is when a friend is in trouble and there's something you can do to help.* But when she looked about her there was no one there but herself and Jean-Pierre, finishing off his salad.

And now that she had decided, she had the most frightening thought of all. What if she were too late? How long had she been sitting there since she had so rudely shouted at the old man and fled. She snatched up Jean-Pierre and ran out of the glen.

Her mother and father were standing in the doorway of the farm-house, their arms about one another's waists. They were looking after Mr Flippo who was shambling over to where his car was parked. The burden of his troubles seemed to weigh upon him so that he looked like a walking question mark with a too-small hat sitting on top of its head.

'Wait! Oh, please wait!' Cecile shouted at the top of her lungs. But the wind must have been in the wrong direction, for he did not hear her. He reached the car and slowly, as though all his limbs were paining him, climbed into it. Holding tight to Jean-Pierre, Cecile went tearing down the hill as fast as ever she could run. But by the time she reached the drive, the old machine was wheezing off.

Cecile cried, 'Come back, Mr Flippo!' and waved wildly at him with her free hand. Tears were streaming down her face. 'Won't you please come back, Mr Flippo!'

The rattles, bangs, hisses and chugs of the ancient car drowned her voice. But in his cracked, rear-vision mirror, Mr Flippo caught a glimpse of the small, unhappy figure and the frantically waving arm. He stopped, and backed to where Cecile was standing. Her parents had come down from the house to find out what all the shouting was about.

He leaned from the window of his car and apologized to her. 'Forgive me for leaving without saying good-bye to you. But I thought you were so angry with me, you would not wish to see me any more.'

'Mr Flippo,' Cecile said, going to him and holding out the Guinea Pig, 'I won't sell you Jean-Pierre. I'll GIVE him to you.'

'What's that you're saying?'

'I'll give him to you for Angelique. Here, take him.'

Mr Flippo opened the door of the old rattle-trap and climbed out, and stood looking down upon Cecile with a wonderful new light in his eyes. But he said, 'Cecile, are you sure? Have you thought carefully? Do you know what you are doing?'

'Yes, I have. Please take him. I know you'll be kind to him.' And she thrust Jean-Pierre into his hands.

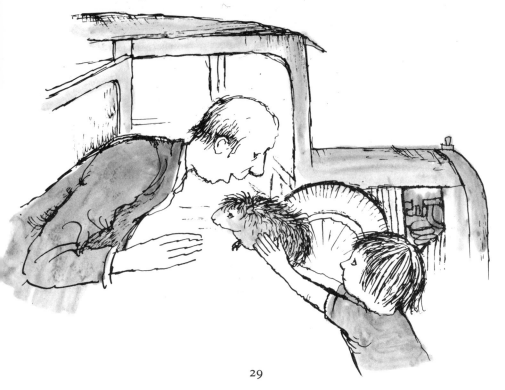

For an instant Mr Flippo regarded the small bundle of fur sitting up in his palms sneezing, once, twice, thrice and four times. And suddenly, shrill and loud came Mr Flippo's laughter: 'Tee-hee-hee. Tee-hee-hee-hee-hee. Tee-hee-heeeee!'

All three stared at him in astonishment.

'Clowns are always supposed to laugh when they are crying, aren't they?' he said.

They looked and saw that although the eyes were no longer sad, they were indeed filled with tears.

CHAPTER V

FROM THE moment of Flippo's safe arrival back at Tarbes early the next morning, everything went most marvellously.

The reunion between Angelique and Jean-Pierre was a happy and touching one and thereafter the magic of Jean-Pierre was at its best.

They recognized one another immediately. At the first glimpse of the Guinea Pig, Angelique bounded high into the air with joy and then sniffed and snuffled and kissed him. And when Flippo popped him once more into her pouch, tears moistened her eyes. For kangaroos are rather gentle and sensitive creatures and Angelique was particularly so.

The other members of the small and rather miserable circus crowded around. They were cheered by the sight and marvelled and made a fuss over them.

Michel Frenet, the owner, came around to see what the noise was all about and, incidentally, to sack Flippo. But seeing Angelique with Jean-Pierre's head sticking out of her pouch, he roared with laughter instead. He clapped the old clown on the shoulder and said, 'There you are, my friend! You've taken my advice! Well, that's really original. We ought to pack 'em in. We

need not speak further about your leaving us just yet.'

What a relief for Pasquini-Flippo! The immediate threat of being out of a job and on the street was removed. Nevertheless, his business sense did not desert him and he said, 'Monsieur Frenet, don't you think perhaps now a contract might be in order?'

But while, as Flippo had said, Frenet was a good enough fellow, his business sense did not desert him either. At that particular moment it was a fatal mistake. He said, 'Plenty of time to talk about that later, when we see how things go. In the meantime, you are to continue at your old salary. I will tell my wife to fix up a hat for the little fellow and won't charge you for it.'

The clown was in no mood to argue at this point and merely said, 'Oh, thank you, Monsieur.'

'That's quite all right,' said the circus owner. 'Where did you find him and what do you call him?'

Flippo replied to the second question but not to the first. 'His name is Jean-Pierre. He's an Abyssinian Guinea Pig.' Whereupon Jean-Pierre, hearing his name, sneezed again enthusiastically, popping in and out of the pouch, while Angelique gazed down upon him fondly.

'Abyssinian, you say?' queried Frenet. 'Great! Wonderful! That makes it even better. I'll have some new posters of the pair made up immediately, and we'll send them on ahead of us. That ought to do the trick.'

And indeed it did.

Jean-Pierre's magic, or the attraction of a brand new star turn, call it what you will, worked wonders. The coloured posters sent on in advance and stuck up on the sides of barns or in the village squares, caught the attention of everyone. No one in France had ever seen such a thing as a genuine Australian kangaroo containing an equally genuine Abyssinian Guinea Pig. Thus, when the little circus paused on its northward journey, there was hardly ever an empty seat. Flippo worked up a marvellously amusing routine.

Jean-Pierre learned his part very quickly. Things began to look up for the small travelling circus.

But this was only the beginning of Flippo's good fortune. For when they reached the city of Bordeaux, a stout man wearing a fancy waistcoat, bowler hat and a large diamond ring on his little finger, came around to the clown tent after the performance. Flippo was removing his makeup with Jean-Pierre in his lap. The two men had a long discussion. They kept their voices low, so that no one could hear the subject of their talk. When they had finished, the stout man produced a piece of paper which Flippo signed. Then the pair shook hands.

When the stranger departed, Flippo went directly to the wagon of Monsieur Frenet. There he said, 'Monsieur, I regret to have to inform you that at the end of the week I am leaving your circus.'

'What?' cried the owner. 'Leave? Just when you are a success again? But I said you could remain.'

'Oh yes, that's true,' said Flippo, 'but when I asked you for a contract, you put me off. Nor did you offer to pay me any more money. Do you remember?'

'Oh, la!' snorted Frenet, 'What need is there of a contract between friends? But if you insist, I will have one written up, and we might even perhaps discuss a slight increase in salary.'

'That's very kind, I'm sure,' said the comic, and he was unable to conceal his satisfaction at what he now had to tell. 'But I'm afraid it's too late. I have just signed a two-year contract with one of the Bouglione brothers at five times what you are paying me. I am to have my own wagon with proper space for Angelique as well, and we are to be one of the star turns, with my name advertised in large letters.'

And that was the beginning of the most wonderful time of all, for Flippo, Angelique and Jean-Pierre. For there were at that time two great travelling circuses in Europe: the Family Knie of Switzerland and the Bouglione Brothers of Italy. It was with the latter that Flippo and his novel, trained kangaroo act had finally struck it rich.

This was no tatty little show with broken down machinery and tired animals, but a great, glittering collection of wonderful artists and splendid beasts. They performed in huge towns and big cities in an enormous tent, to the music of their own gaily-attired band.

Everything was different even from the circus in which Flippo had played in Australia. The costumes were fresh and gay; the horses sleek, shining and the finest ever. There were lions and tigers, elephants and the zoo even boasted a giraffe.

Jean-Pierre was thrilled by the glitter and the noise, the cracking of whips, the firing of pistols, the shouts of the clowns and the roars of delight that greeted his appearance. No wonder that his head was slightly turned and that he rarely thought of the flower farm back in Cannes and his secret place in the cellar with Cecile.

Flippo gave Jean-Pierre all his favourite foods and pomegranate seeds every other day. They had a red and gold motor caravan with Flippo's name painted in blue letters on the outside.

They were heading for Paris where the Bougliones had taken over the *Cirque Metropole* for the autumn and winter season. This was a theatre specially built for circuses. And by the time they

got there, Monsieur Pasquini now looking neither stooped, nor old, nor grey, was well back on his feet once more. He had a good watch, a new camera, and above all, a glittering traditional clown costume sewn with thousands of coloured sequins. Only the very best and highest paid artists can afford such.

But of all of this Cecile knew not a single, solitary thing. Although the star turn of Flippo, Angelique and Jean-Pierre was a sensation in the circus world, no word of this trickled back to the journals of the Riviera.

But what, then, was the trouble with Flippo? Why had he not written? He could have sent Cecile photographs he had taken of Jean-Pierre and Angelique, of the wagon and of the poster with his name in letters three feet high. He could even have telephoned her, to report on his splendid success.

Often Flippo had been on the verge of doing one or the other, or all of these things. Yet, each time in the last moment he had not done so. For all of his comeback, the person behind Flippo—Monsieur Pasquini—was not able to forget that he had been an old man on the point of being discarded and turned loose to starve. The two-year contract in his pocket did not crackle so loudly that it drowned out the memories of his narrow escape. Deep down he was just a little afraid that Cecile might ask for Jean-Pierre back. He excused this cowardice by saying to himself that to keep reminding Cecile of Jean-Pierre and her sacrifice, would be more cruel than that he and her one-time pet should disappear out of her life.

And in one respect Flippo was quite right. Cecile missed Jean-Pierre dreadfully. Once the glow resulting from the knowledge that she had done something that was good and helpful had worn off, she found that the departure of Jean-Pierre had left a great gap in her life. She discovered that it was one thing to do a noble deed and make a genuine sacrifice and another to have to live with it afterwards.

But of this, Cecile thought, her parents knew nothing. She was certain that she had concealed her feelings when she had gone back to the house to fetch Jean-Pierre's travelling box down from the attic. She had handed it through the window of the old car, with instructions as to feeding, care and brushing. At his leave-taking, Monsieur Pasquini had held out Jean-Pierre to her for a final good-bye.

She had taken him, kissed him and handed him back quickly. She had wanted to say, 'Don't forget me, Jean-Pierre, or your magic,' but did not. That was the kind of thing one said only in secret and not before grownups.

The Guinea Pig had sneezed and then struggled a little in her hands, not because she had kissed him, but because his eye had caught a glimpse of the travelling box and he was not particularly eager to get into it again. But he had calmed down when returned once more to the man, who deposited him gently inside. He had curled up in the straw and decided to go to sleep.

On the way back to the house, Monsieur Durand had suddenly put an arm about her shoulder and squeezed her to him, saying, 'I'm very proud of you, Cecile.'

She pretended at first that she did not know what he was talking about. But when he had added, 'That is a very good and kind thing you have done,' she quickly changed the subject, for fear she might cry.

'Oh,' she had said, 'wasn't Jean-Pierre funny when he didn't want to go into his box? Do you suppose he remembered?'

She would rather have died than have them find out that sometimes now she went down to the cellar, where she used to feed Jean-Pierre. In the dead quiet, since now there was no rustling in straw, or squeaking, or sneezing, or clicking of teeth, she often wept to herself for her lost companion.

For she was discovering that with his departure he seemed to have taken away all the glamour and magic from their secret places. The barn, the cellar, the glen on the side of the hill and their particular, gnarled old olive tree that Cecile had been able to climb and imagine herself in a fairy house, had become quite ordinary.

In the past Cecile had told Jean-Pierre everything there—her joys, her worries, her troubles and her thoughts. It could have been about a bad day at school, a scolding when she had irritated her mother, a treat in store, or a disappointment of some sort or another. Or they would have had just plain conversation about things. She whispered into his pink ear and was rewarded with grunts, or teeth clickings, or happy sneezes. It was no fun to go to these places any more, for there was no longer any sharing.

Of course Cecile was quite wrong when she thought that her father and mother had not noticed how much she missed Jean-Pierre. For if young people are inclined to be secretive, parents are too. They do not tell their children everything they think or have noticed. Instead they talk it over between themselves when they are alone at night, and try to decide what to do for the best.

Madame Durand was well aware of Cecile's little trips to the cellar. Sobs sometimes have a way of penetrating even through closed doors. Monsieur Durand had observed that Jean-Pierre's cage had been removed from the barn. Also his daughter was unusually quiet and thoughtful in the evenings when she was at the dinner table. Instead of trying to remain as long as she could chattering, now they had hardly finished the pudding course when she was up and away to her room.

The Durands also thought it very odd that not a single solitary word had been received from Mr Flippo. They had supposed him to be a gentle and kindly man with an understanding of human beings and especially children. He would surely realize what a great gesture their daughter had made when she had handed over her pet. Why had he not at least sent a postcard? Two months had now gone by since his departure.

Monsieur Durand would have written to Pasquini to enquire, but he did not know any address. There was no point in sending a letter to Tarbes, for the Cirque Frenet would long since have vanished into the blue and in all likelihood would be across the border into Belgium, Holland or Germany.

Cecile was not a child who was inclined either to mope or moan. Her parents were certain that eventually she would recover from the parting. They had been sufficiently wise as not to suggest that perhaps she might like to have another Guinea Pig. For they knew that Jean-Pierre had occupied a special place in the heart of their daughter. It was the uncertainty that was so upsetting. Were Mr Flippo, his Angelique and in particular, Jean-Pierre alive or dead?

None of the family was prepared for the astonishing manner in which this question was to be answered.

CHAPTER VI

IT BEGAN one dark, rainy November evening when Cecile had already retired to her room. Monsieur Durand was thumbing through the weekly television programmes, wondering whether there was anything worth while. Suddenly he shouted, 'Ha!' and then, 'Well, well!' and struck the page with the back of his hand in excitement.

Madame Durand looked up from her tapestry in some alarm. Her husband arose, went over and showed her the photograph and the text on the printed page.

'There,' he said, 'what do you think of that?' Then, looking at his watch he added, 'We're just in time.' He glanced in the direction of the stairs leading above and said, 'Cecile! We must break the rule.'

'Oh yes, indeed we must,' replied Madame Durand.

'Then go and fetch her, while I turn on the programme.'

For it was firmly established in the Durand household that homework came first. Cecile never looked at television in the evenings, but only at weekends and on holidays. Her father must have come upon something very special to suggest that this strict routine be altered.

He had indeed.

When Cecile's mother knocked at the door of her daughter's room (another rule in the Durand household was that people always knocked on doors before entering), she found that Cecile had already put her books away. Apparently she had been sitting at her desk, staring in front of her. When she had finished her work, Cecile often enjoyed just dreaming or imagining things before she undressed. Then she would take the imaginings to bed with her and they would send her off to sleep.

'Homework finished already?' Madame Durand asked.

Cecile replied, 'Yes. I didn't have much to do tonight.'

'Good,' said her mother. 'Would you like to come down and look at a television programme with us—just this once for a treat?'

This was indeed a surprise and Cecile jumped up eagerly. 'Oh yes, please, may I? What is it?'

Madame Durand did not wish to give away the secret, so she just said, 'Papa seems to have found something special he thought you would like.'

Cecile and her mother arrived in the living room just as, with the blare of music, the picture locked into place on the screen. It announced itself as, 'La Piste aux Etoiles', which means, 'The Stage of the Stars'. This was a famous French programme shown every two weeks, devoted to the finest circus performers on the continent and broadcast from Paris.

'Oh goody, goody, a circus!' cried Cecile and settled herself on the floor to enjoy it. Since Jean-Pierre had gone away, everything connected with this form of entertainment interested her.

The television camera seemed to be right inside the ring, so that one really had the most wonderful view just as though one were sitting in the very front row.

The band struck up a fanfare; and the show began with a juggler on a unicycle who was followed by a troupe of Hungarian tumblers in gay costumes. There was a group of trained elephants and a most beautiful girl in shimmering tights who performed on a high trapeze, her spangles flashing in the spotlights. Then came trained ponies and liberty horses and afterwards a man who balanced on a high, swaying pole held by his partner.

There followed a moment of pause, broken by a long roll upon the drums. The ringmaster stepped forward to the centre and gazed about the audience. Cecile suddenly had the funniest feeling in the pit of her stomach.

The ringmaster announced: 'And now, ladies and gentlemen, La Piste des Etoiles takes great pride in presenting the star turn of this evening. For the first time on television, we introduce the

41

latest world-famous, comedy sensation—Flippo, Angelique and Jean-Pierre!'

Over the loud fanfare of the band came the sound of the honking of one of those old-fashioned, rubber-bulb motor-car horns. Into the arena drove a caravan with windows in it like a little house. A crooked chimney pipe stuck up from the roof and on the sides, in curlicue circus letters each a foot high, was written: 'FLIPPO, ANGELIQUE AND JEAN-PIERRE', and in much smaller letters, '*Cirque Bouglione*'. At the wheel sat the clown himself.

But what a different Flippo! His face was hidden behind chalk white makeup. A big, red nose was stuck on over his own long,

thin one, and a wide, red mouth split in a grin, had been painted from ear to ear. He was most magnificently clad in the traditional suit of tight pantaloons and jacket, covered with flashing sequins.

'Honk, honk, honk!' went the horn, 'Bang, bang, bang!' went three backfires like pistol shots, as the vehicle came to a halt in the centre of the ring, to thunderous applause.

'Papa!' screamed Cecile, 'It really *is* Mr Flippo!'

43

Flippo dismounted and threw open two side doors, and hippety-hop, and huppety-hup, a kangaroo bounded into the ring. On her head she wore a white clown's hat and around her neck a ruff.

Cecile screamed again, 'There's Angelique, but where's Jean-Pierre?' For an instant she entertained the dreadful thought that something might have happened to him and that he was no longer with them.

'Wait!' said her father.

Flippo pretended in pantomime to have lost something. He searched inside the caravan for a moment. He looked all about himself. He turned his pockets inside out and peered up his sleeves. Nothing!

Not finding what he seemed to be searching for, he turned his

back upon Angelique and gave a shrug of despair. As he did so, a great shout of laughter went up from the audience. For while the clown was not looking, there, popping out of the pouch of the kangaroo, a tiny clown hat fastened onto the top of his shaggy head, was . . .

'Jean-Pierre! Jean-Pierre!' cried Cecile, and hardly knowing what she was doing, was on her knees in front of the set, her fingers touching the glass of the screen. 'Oh, Mama, Papa, look! It's Jean-Pierre!' And then addressing the set she cried, 'Oh, Jean-Pierre, Jean-Pierre, how are you? I've missed you so!' But, naturally, there was no reply since the Guinea Pig was miles away in Paris and at that moment engaged with his act.

This consisted of sticking his head out of Angelique's pouch when Flippo's back was to him and slipping down out of sight when he turned around, with the audience screaming and shouting with delight at Flippo's discomfiture.

But at last the clown whipped about too fast for the Guinea Pig to conceal himself and the shrill, 'Tee-hee-hee-hee-hee-hee-heeee!' of his characteristic laughter rang through the arena as he pointed and said, 'Oh, there you are, you little rascal!' Removing him from Angelique's pouch, he held him up for all the audience to see. The television set in the Durand living-room rattled to the thunder of applause.

Cecile screamed, 'Jean-Pierre!' again, and reached out, trying to touch him. But of course there was only the glass of the picture tube.

Flippo restored the Guinea Pig to Angelique's pouch, whereupon the kangaroo gave him a kiss and then went through her routine of tricks. She balanced a huge ball on the end of her nose. She rode a tricycle. She skipped with a rope. Cecile had no eyes for Flippo or even the cleverness of Angelique, but only for that tiny face under the miniature clown hat, peering forth from the pocket in the kangaroo's stomach.

And now for the climax of the act. Flippo removed Jean-Pierre from Angelique's pouch and set him down onto the ground, sitting up on his hind legs. From inside the caravan he produced a large sign which read, 'Referee', which he placed behind Jean-Pierre. Then he brought out two pairs of boxing gloves; one he put on Angelique's front paws and the other he wore himself. The ringmaster blew a shrill whistle and Flippo and Angelique began to box. Jean-Pierre looked from one to the other, wrinkling up his nose, clicking his teeth and sneezing.

Slappety-slap, thuppety-thup went the gloves, as the clown and the kangaroo thumped one another merrily. Once, as Flippo spun around, Angelique gave him a seemingly hard kick with one of her powerful hind legs, so that he sprawled into the sawdust. Jean-Pierre went over to him where he lay and seemed to be whispering something into his ear, as the drummer tolled off the count with thumps of his drumstick—two, three, four, five . . .

After the count had reached ten, Flippo did not rise but continued to lie there, while Angelique's 'victory' was greeted with cheers.

The ringmaster went over to Flippo, lifted him up and helped him to his feet. The clown had his hands clasped to his chest, and his legs for a moment did not seem quite steady. But then he straightened up, went over to Angelique, shook hands with her, and raised his hat to the audience. He picked up Jean-Pierre and held him high in the air to receive his share of the crowd's approval.

'Was something the matter?' Cecile asked. 'Was Mr Flippo hurt?'

'No, no,' replied Monsieur Durand, 'that's all a part of the act, of course. He was just pretending.'

Indeed that seemed to be the case, for now, laughing his absurd, 'Tee-hee-hee-hee-hee-heeee', he popped Jean-Pierre back inside Angelique and gave her a bit of something out of his pocket to nibble as a treat. Of her own accord she hopped back into the caravan. After closing the doors, Flippo resumed the driver's seat and honking his horn and backfiring, he drove triumphantly around the ring, bowing and raising his cap until he disappeared behind the exit curtains.

When the show was over, they all sat and talked about it. They discussed just what Flippo had done here and Angelique there, and how Jean-Pierre had practically stolen the show. It seemed hardly possible that only a few months before, a beaten old man had sat in that very room with them, and now there he had been, a star of the biggest circus in Paris.

'You should be very proud of Jean-Pierre,' her father said to Cecile. And indeed she was. She could hardly wait to go to school the next day, for she was certain that many of her schoolmates would have seen the show and Jean-Pierre. They would, of course, remember him.

But for all her pride and joy at seeing her pet once more under such marvellous circumstances, Cecile was aware of an under-lying feeling of bewilderment and hurt. For she had been taught

47

by her parents that the first thing one did when one had been given a present or been invited out, was to sit down and write a letter. As the star of *La Piste aux Etoiles*, Mr Flippo must surely now be rich and successful. And yet he had never once thought to write to her and tell her how Jean-Pierre was faring and perhaps even say 'Thank you.'

CHAPTER VII

NOT EVEN the excitement of her school friends the following day could quite make up to Cecile for the sadness she felt at not hearing from Mr Flippo and Jean-Pierre.

Practically all the girls and some of her teachers as well, had seen Jean-Pierre the night before. *La Piste aux Etoiles* was a popular programme and Cecile found herself something of a heroine. She had to repeat the story many times of the unexpected appearance of Mr Flippo on their farm doorstep, his problem and how it had been solved. To her credit, she did it with modesty and as though there had really been nothing else for her to do but to help Mr Flippo.

Nevertheless, Cecile found it pleasant to be a sensation at her school for a day. Even the mistresses were interested and remarked to her about Jean-Pierre. All through the lunchtime break, she was surrounded by her classmates chattering about the exciting event.

'Wasn't Flippo funny when he couldn't find Jean-Pierre, and he was inside Angelique all the time?'

'How clever of Jean-Pierre to know when to pop up at just the right time. Did you teach him that, Cecile?'

'I thought Angelique was sweet. I wish I had a kangaroo.'

'Oh, I do too,' said Cecile. Since she had seen Angelique she found herself wishing that she, too, could own such a strange yet sweet and gentle creature. 'We could keep her in our barn.'

'What would you give her to eat?'

'Oh, spinachy things, I suppose,' Cecile replied. 'I could look it up. And then Jean-Pierre could live inside her all the time.'

'I'd like to have a caravan like that,' said another of her friends.

'Oh, so would I!' cried Cecile, for *that* thought had not been far from her mind either. 'If we had one like that we could play circus with it, with Jean-Pierre and Angelique. And after that, we could cook our supper in it, or bake a cake.'

For those are always the dreams of children and, for that matter, of grownups too, after they have seen a circus. They imagine themselves in the roles of the wonderful people of the show, living what would seem to be the most exciting lives in the world.

And this was expressed by another of Cecile's playmates. 'Jean-Pierre must be having the most wonderful time. Have you heard from him? It must be marvellous, travelling with a circus.'

This was the question that Cecile had been dreading. But she managed to answer it without exactly telling a fib. 'Oh, he's loving it.' For she felt sure that it was so.

'Maybe some day Flippo will come in his caravan to visit you. Could we all come and see him?'

This was an idea, too, which had been on Cecile's mind and she had thought how splendid such a thing would be. Yet, at the same time something in her heart seemed to tell her that if he had never bothered to write, he would not come either.

She replied, 'Oh yes, of course,' and put as good a face to it as she could, to hide the fact that both Mr Flippo and Jean-Pierre had forgotten her.

50

The day passed between pleasure and heartache, and when she arrived home that night, she was more than usually silent. She went down to the cellar and the empty archway. There, where she used to feed Jean-Pierre and have most of her secret talks with him, she had a good cry.

But having done so and felt better for it, she pulled herself together. For Cecile was not a girl to give in to feeling sorry for herself.

She had made the gift of Jean-Pierre of her own free will and no strings attached. And, she told herself, if Mr Flippo was too busy to write to her, now that she had an address, there was nothing to prevent her writing to him.

So that evening when she had done her homework, she sat down and wrote a letter to Monsieur Pasquini (Mr Flippo), Stage of the Stars, Radio-Télévision Française, Paris.

'Dear Mr Flippo,

'How are you? And how is Jean-Pierre? We saw you on Television last night and you were wonderful. I thought Angelique was sweet and am glad that Jean-Pierre has such a kind friend. I thought your costume was beautiful. All my friends at school saw the show and thought you were wonderful. I would love to meet Angelique one day. My friends in school wished they had a kangaroo, because she looked so sweet and gentle, and I would too. I hope I can meet her some day.

'I have passed my exam in history with a good mark, but did not do so well in maths. Is Jean-Pierre behaving himself? I know you are very busy but if you have a moment, I would love to have a letter from you and Jean-Pierre.

'Your loving friend,
Cecile.'

After she had addressed and sealed the envelope, Cecile went to her mother for a stamp and it did not take much guesswork on the part of the Durands to know that she had written to Mr Flippo.

Monsieur Durand thought how clever and unselfish of his daughter. It also saved him the trouble of writing himself, as he had intended to do, including one or two sharp sentences on what sort of a way was this to treat a child.

Monsieur Durand told himself he was not the kind of person to put up with anything that affected the happiness of Cecile. He did not know to what extent his praiseworthy emotion was about to be put to the test.

The letter was posted the following morning, on the way to school. Allowing a day or so for it to reach Paris, plus the delay in forwarding it to whatever address they had for Pasquini, it would be at least a week before any reply might be expected.

Thereafter, as the postman arrived after Cecile had left for school, Monsieur Durand would leaf through the mail quickly to see if there was something for her. And when Cecile came home at night, she would give what seemed to be only the most casual glance to the place on the side table in the hall, where post for her was usually left.

The week passed with no letter. Each day suspense and hope would be built up only to be shattered. The longer it went on and the deeper the mystery, the more impossible it became for anyone to raise the subject.

Until one peaceful evening at the flower farm the answer to it all exploded violently in the cosy living-room.

Cecile was about to go up to do her homework. Madame Durand was taking her tapestry from her work bag. And Monsieur Durand was just settling down to catch up with last Sunday's news-paper, the *Nice Matin*, which he had not yet had time to read, when the telephone rang.

With a groan Monsieur Durand heaved himself up out of his chair to answer it. Cecile and her mother could hear clearly the operator saying, 'Hello? Monsieur Durand? A personal call from Paris. Hold the line please.'

'Yes, yes, speaking. Who is calling me from Paris?'

There was a click in the telephone and then another voice saying, 'Monsieur Durand? One moment, please, Monsieur Ricardo Bouglione would like a word with you.'

Monsieur Durand said, 'What? What? Bouglione?' And then, turning to his family he repeated the name, asking, 'Do we know any Bouglione?'

Madame Durand looked blank and so did Cecile. In the hall she already had one foot on the stairs when she suddenly let out a little scream, 'Papa! Wasn't that the name written on the side of the circus wagon? Perhaps it's Mr Flippo!' And she started to run towards the telephone.

Her father energetically waved her to silence. He pressed the receiver more firmly to his ear, for apparently Monsieur Bouglione was now speaking at the other end. From then on Cecile could no longer hear what was being said from Paris during the pauses, but only her father's side of a most dumbfounding conversation.

'Hello, hello? . . . Yes, this is Monsieur Durand . . . Yes, I have a daughter by the name of Cecile . . . Do I know you? . . . Ah, yes, of course, the circus proprietor.'

Almost breathless with excitement, Cecile cried, 'Papa, what is it?' But she was shushed to silence.

'A letter?' he continued. 'No, she has received no letter, at least not yet. Perhaps it will come tomorrow.'

Monsieur Durand then said, 'What?' and then once more, 'What?' in a louder voice and then with a stunned expression on his face, 'You say Mr Flippo is dead? . . . A heart attack?'

Madame Durand arose from her chair crying, 'Oh, the poor man!'

Cecile was too frightened to say anything. Mr Flippo dead? How terrible! And of course her next thought was for Jean-Pierre. *Where was he? What was happening to him?*

'No, no,' André Durand was saying, 'I haven't had time yet to look at the Sunday paper. Please accept my condolences. It is good of you to call . . . Oh, yes, I see. It's about my daughter's Guinea Pig.'

'Jean-Pierre!' screamed Cecile and drew another 'Shshsh!' from her father.

'Pasquini left a will? . . . What's that? . . . With immediate instructions as to the animals? . . . You say everything to my daughter? . . . But this is impos—— . . . !'

Cecile watched her father anxiously, trying to guess what it was all about. She saw that her parent had turned first quite pale, then red and finally purple. His hand holding the instrument began to tremble. Even his moustache was quivering. When he spoke again it was no longer in normal tones, but a horrified shout.

'On their way here? But I forbid it! We cannot receive these

54

things! You must stop it! . . . Too late, you say? . . . Departed tonight? But this is an imposition! . . . Blast the wretched animals! How could you have permitted such a thing! . . . At ten tomorrow morning? In Nice? . . . I don't know what to say, Monsieur Bouglione! This is a bombshell! I'm numb.'

And numbed indeed he was. For he simply let fall the telephone receiver into its cradle, cutting the connection. Half in a daze he mumbled, 'Jean-Pierre is on his way here.'

'Oh Papa! Papa!' screamed Cecile. 'How? When?'

Her father turned his shocked gaze upon his family, 'Inside Angelique.'

It was now the part of Madame Durand to look slightly alarmed. 'Inside Angelique? But I don't understand. Coming here?'

The bewildered man held both hands to his head, 'In her cage.

They will be arriving on the *auto-couchette* train from Paris, at Nice, at ten o'clock tomorrow morning.'

'Goodness me,' said Cecile's mother, 'you mean to say they've put those poor animals in a draughty cage on one of those trains on which they transport cars?'

'No, no, no!' groaned Monsieur Durand, with his eyes now lifted towards heaven. 'The cage is inside the caravan—the private circus wagon of poor Mr Flippo. He was seized with a heart attack last Friday night, and died. But it seems that there was a letter of instructions and a will. He has left all that he had: the kangaroo, Jean-Pierre, the caravan and everything in it to Cecile.'

'To me?' cried Cecile, wild with excitement. 'Oh, Mummy, how wonderful!!!'

CHAPTER VIII

'But it's impossible! I tell you, it's completely and utterly unthinkable! This is a flower farm and not a zoo,' growled Monsieur Durand, as he leafed frantically through the *Nice Matin* of the Sunday before. Cecile and her mother crowded around to help him look.

'Ha! Here it is,' and he read the item to them out loud:

'Children of Paris and elsewhere will mourn the unexpected passing of Marcel Pasquini, better known as the clown Flippo, who with his educated kangaroo Angelique and trained Guinea Pig Jean-Pierre, has brought joy and laughter to thousands of youthful hearts.

'Monsieur Pasquini complained of feeling ill after the Friday night performance, but recovered sufficiently to go home to his flat at No. 6, Rue Jambonier, in the ninth *arrondissement*, Paris. He was discovered on Saturday morning by the wife of Monsieur

Lenoir the concierge, having apparently died of a heart attack in his sleep.

'Monsieur Pasquini had no family or relatives. Though successful in a recent come-back, he was not wealthy, and at the moment it is not known what disposition is to be made of his effects and his trained animals. Monsieur Ricardo Bouglione, managing director of the Bouglione Circus now performing at the Cirque Metropole, and where Monsieur Pasquini was engaged, declared that the animals, of course, would be well looked after until it was determined what should be done with them.

'The late Monsieur Pasquini, or Flippo, was recently seen by millions on television on *La Piste aux Etoiles* programme. The *Nice Matin* joins the many who will regret the passing of this talented and beloved clown.'

'Ha!' shouted Monsieur Durand again, when he had finished and then repeated, ' "Monsieur Bouglione . . . declared that the animals would be well looked after", and so he simply sent off the whole caboosh to me! Well, I tell you I won't have it!'

'Oh Papa, *please!*' pleaded Cecile, 'Can't we have Angelique? And we could play circus with the caravan.' For sad as was the sudden passing of Mr Flippo, she could not help but see herself the owner of a genuine circus wagon, entertaining her friends. 'It wouldn't be in the way.'

'Certainly not!' replied her father. 'We cannot keep a kangaroo here. What is it that we know about kangaroos? Nothing! It is a wild animal and perhaps savage. How would I explain its presence to our neighbours? They would laugh at us! And as for a circus wagon, I suppose you would wish to draw it up in front of the driveway for everyone to gape at, as though we were gypsies!'

'But what will you do?' Madame Durand asked. 'It will be here in the morning.'

'Do, do, do!' repeated Monsieur Durand who was now thoroughly annoyed. 'Something, I tell you. I don't know what. But it cannot stay here!'

Cecile tried once more. 'But Papa, I would look after her. I promise you'd hardly ever notice her.'

'Of course,' said Monsieur Durand, 'and I suppose you'll give up school, so that you will be here all day long to see to Angelique's wants? You'll have your Jean-Pièrre back and that should satisfy you. Everything else must be got rid of immediately. We will offer the kangaroo to the Zoological Gardens of His Highness Prince Rainier of Monaco. I'm sure that he'll be most pleased to receive it. As for the caravan, we'll sell it as quickly as possible and—ah —I'll put the money into the bank for you.'

For he had suddenly remembered that actually, everything had been left to his daughter and he was rather high-handedly disposing of them. But he was too angry and upset to give much further thought to this.

Poor Cecile had never been in such a muddle. She did not know whether to laugh or cry. She was overjoyed that her beloved Jean-Pierre was to be returned to her. She wanted to weep over the sad, lonely death of Mr Flippo. And she did not know how to contain her disappointment over her father's decision.

She merely begged, 'May I come with you to Nice tomorrow, to meet . . . Angelique and fetch Jean-Pierre?'

'No, you may not!' replied her father severely, 'You will go to school in the morning as usual and no nonsense. I will bring Jean-Pierre home with me.'

Cecile was so frightened by his stern tone that she said nothing. But Madame Durand quite gently remarked, 'But you know, André, tomorrow is Thursday and Cecile has no school. It wouldn't do any harm, really for her to . . .'

'Oh well, then, all right,' he said, for he felt a bit of a fool at having forgotten that in France children have Thursdays free during the week, and instead go to school all day Saturday. 'But now I suggest, perhaps, we'd best all go to bed.'

58

That night Cecile hardly slept for excitement. She would see Jean-Pierre in the morning. And before *they* went to sleep that night, Monsieur Durand had a further talk with his wife in no uncertain terms. Like all grown-ups, Madame Durand was engaged at the idea of an inheritance and mentioned what a pity it was that the first time anyone had actually been left anything in their family, they could not keep it. Cecile would have had such pleasure out of it.

'Keep it, indeed!' her husband had replied indignantly. 'If someone were to will you an elephant, would you insist upon chaining it up amongst our glass-houses? If you were left an entire circus, I suppose you would expect me to give up our farm, wear a check suit and take it on the road!'

'I suppose you are right, André,' said his wife. 'Although a kangaroo doesn't seem like a great deal . . .'

'It is enough!' said her husband angrily. 'Not to mention being saddled with a caravan, sent off without so much as a by-your-leave. Typical of show people; heedless, thoughtless and irresponsible!'

'I was only thinking of Cecile,' said his wife.

But this set Monsieur Durand off again. 'Haven't we had enough trouble already with that wretched Guinea Pig of hers? Can you imagine what our lives would be like with a kangaroo? Once and for all. NO!'

Monsieur Durand had quite forgotten that not so long ago he had thought of himself as one who would not put up with anything that might affect the happiness of his daughter.

The following morning before they started off for Nice in the farm van, the delayed letter from Mr Flippo, sent before he had died, arrived. It read:

'My dear Cecile,
'I am writing this to you as my best friend. I feel that I am

gravely ill and perhaps have not many hours more to remain here. But you must not be sad, for you have made the end of my life the happiest and most successful time that I have ever known. I am prepared with joy and contentment to meet what is to come.

'I have not much in this world except my beloved Angelique and her I send to you, with a few things that I own, such as my caravan, my press cuttings and some gifts I have received from time to time; all that will remain by which to remember Mr Flippo. My clown costume I have directed to be sold, since it is quite valuable and will defray all expenses, and therefore no burden will be put upon you or your family.

'From the love you lavished upon our little Guinea Pig, Jean-Pierre, I know that you will take the best care of Angelique, and that she and Jean-Pierre will remain happy friends together, as they have in the past.

'I am sorry I did not write to you before. I was a cowardly old man who was afraid that you might ask to have Jean-Pierre back and I would lose all the money, glitter and the comfort of success which, as I write now, I know is as nothing. And so to to try to make it up, I give you Angelique.

'I have also written a note to my friend Monsieur Ricardo Bouglione, to say that if some morning I should not wake up, he must without any delay, see that my wishes are carried out and my caravan containing Angelique, Jean-Pierre, my love and gratitude, be despatched to you forthwith.

'Yours ever with eternal thankfulness,
'Marcel Pasquini (Mr Flippo).'

And at the very bottom of the letter he had written, 'Tee-hee-hee-hee-hee-hee-heeeeee!'

The letter was most touching and Monsieur Durand felt genuinely sorry for the old circus clown. But he was still greatly put out and now further irritated by the reminder that this was a legacy. All these things had been left to Cecile and therefore were not even his to sell or give away.

Yet Cecile did not mention this, for she knew that when grown-ups lost their tempers and became angry, they were inclined to forget their sense of justice. That is how they were and there was no use complaining when it happened. Besides which he was her father. And so with good grace she bade good-bye to a beautiful dream. It was that of being the only girl in Cannes, and for that matter perhaps in all France, to possess a magic Guinea Pig, a live kangaroo and a real circus caravan. Perhaps once in a while her parents might take her and Jean-Pierre to the Principality of Monaco to visit Angelique in the Zoo.

When they arrived at the railway yards, the Paris train had not yet come in and they had to wait. At last there was a chuff-chuff-chuff in the distance which grew louder, along with the clanging of the engine bell and the long procession of steel, openwork wagons drew into the platform. Each one carried a car resting on it and right smack in the centre of the line of Peugeots, Citroens, Jaguars, Simcas, Fiats and Austins was the most startling creation.

It was the same motorized caravan that they had all seen on the television show. But since the pictures on the screen had been in black and white, none of them had realized or even thought of its gaudy colours. It was painted a bright gold with red wheels and

red roof, and the curlicue letters on its side advertising, 'FLIPPO, ANGELIQUE AND JEAN-PIERRE', and 'Cirque Bouglione' were ultra-marine blue. There was no doubt about it. It was an eye-catcher. As the train drew to a halt, everyone in the yards stopped to gape at it.

'Great heavens!' exclaimed Monsieur Durand.

Cecile was beside herself with excitement. 'Oh, Papa! Isn't it beautiful!'

'Beautiful? That?' said her father. 'It's simply ghastly! It must remain here!'

'But how will you get the kangaroo home, then?' enquired his wife. 'You can't leave her at the station to starve until you have word whether the Prince will accept her for his Zoo.'

'Well then, you will have to drive it, while I take the van back. I wouldn't be caught dead in such an affair.'

There was a baggage master there to check the cars and when the gaudy caravan was once more upon the ground, he turned to Monsieur Durand to ask, 'You have a letter, I believe, from the Circus?'

Cecile's father produced the one from Flippo.

The baggage master said, '*Bien*, Monsieur,' and that was that.

'My Guinea Pig! May I have him now?' Cecile cried.

There was an attendant who evidently had been looking after the beasts, for he opened the double door in the side of the caravan. There was a cage and seated in it together, on their hind legs, were a medium-sized kangaroo and a shaggy, black and brown, golden-eyed, Abyssinian Guinea Pig.

'Jean-Pierre!' Cecile screamed with delight, 'Oh, please, may I have him?'

'But of course,' said the attendant and letting down a ramp leading into the caravan, he opened the cage.

'Cecile, be careful!' But before her father could stop her, she ran up, seized her pet and was cuddling, hugging and kissing him.

This left Monsieur Durand in a perfect position for the astonishing thing that happened next. For he had run over to protect his daughter should the kangaroo be inclined to bite, kick or scratch, or whatever they did when irritated. Thus he was standing on the ground, directly in front of the cage when, with a most tender look in her beautiful, deep, liquid brown eyes, Angelique gave one hop down the ramp, leaned her head forward and kissed him. It was a delicate, slightly damp kiss from the end of her extraordinarily soft, cool and velvety muzzle, deposited upon Monsieur Durand's cheek. The sweetness of this unexpected greeting left him too surprised to move.

CHAPTER IX

'HELLO, HELLO!' commented the attendant, 'she seems to have taken to you. I ain't had any kisses from her on the way down.'

'Ah-hmmm! Well, well!' said Monsieur Durand, and reaching out, patted Angelique on the side of her sleek neck.

That was all she needed. With a melting glance she placed her short front legs about the neck of Monsieur Durand and kissed him again. And then she rested her cheek next to his.

'Well,' said the attendant, 'have a look at that! A regular affair of love at first sight, if ever I saw one.'

'Come, come now!' said Monsieur Durand, for he was becoming slightly self-conscious at Angelique's sudden show of affection, and disengaging her arms from about his neck he said, 'Ahem— Well, it's always been said that I have rather a way with animals. Here, here! Let go! Come, you must stop!'

For Angelique was showing every indication that she wanted to go on cuddling. She had no desire to be parted from Monsieur Durand.

'Oh Papa, see!' exclaimed Cecile, 'She loves you.'

This was indeed most evident to her father's intense embarrassment. The attendants driving the cars were grinning and some of the passengers waiting for their vehicles likewise seemed to be enjoying the spectacle. One of them said to Monsieur Durand, 'You are to be congratulated, sir. You must be a very great trainer of animals indeed, to have them show such affection and happiness at seeing you again.'

Monsieur Durand did not know whether to be pleased or annoyed at being taken for an animal trainer. But the fact was that he had been strangely disconcerted by the greeting that he had received from this creature who had but recently lost her master. Was it indeed true that he had some power over animals? He had seen the kangaroo bestow a kiss upon Flippo in the circus ring

and it had moved him at the time. He was moved now. He replied merely, 'She has a loving nature.'

The crowd that had gathered round was now interfering with the disembarking of the rest of the cars. Madame Durand said anxiously, 'I think we had best be leaving, André, and getting out of the way.'

'Come, Angelique, you must get back into your cage,' ordered Monsieur Durand. He took her by the elbow, somewhat in the manner of one about to help a young lady across the street.

To his great surprise, the kangaroo obeyed docilely with one last, lingering, backward, lovelorn glance that tore at his heart strings.

'If you will drive the van, I will follow with the circus wagon,' Madame Durand said to her husband. 'It should not be too difficult for me.'

'Ah . . . hmmm,' said Monsieur Durand. 'Well now, perhaps you had best take our van home and I'll handle the caravan. You may not be familiar with the gears. And until we have been able to contact the Prince of Monaco, I wouldn't wish anything to happen to the animal.'

And so the procession left the station and headed for the motorway to Cannes. Madame Durand drove slowly, with Cecile next to her holding Jean-Pierre, and Monsieur Durand bringing up the rear.

The excitement and mixture of feelings was nearly too much for Cecile to bear. She wished almost that she had not come. It would have been better, perhaps, if her father had driven Angelique right off to the Palace of Monaco. In a sense it was both cruel and unjust not only to her, but to Jean-Pierre and Angelique to separate them. They would miss one another. And she let out a great sigh. 'Oh Mummy, why can't we keep Angelique?'

'Because,' replied Madame Durand, 'when your father makes up his mind about something, then there's an end to it.'

But when she glanced into her driving mirror to see how her husband was doing she noted that seated in the driver's seat of the circus wagon, he had just returned a courteous salute received from a policeman at a junction. He was also collecting excited waves from the children on the side of the road. And, what was more, to her surprise Monsieur Durand was waving back.

It is well known how quickly news or excitement of any kind carries. A friend of the Durands saw the procession from the window of her house and recognized the family. She telephoned

to another friend who called a neighbour of theirs, who told yet someone else. Thus the word was spread. By the time they arrived home there was a large group of children as well as grown-ups waiting for them.

'Shall we lend you a hand, Monsieur Durand?' asked several.

'No, no thank you,' he replied. He was still uncertain as to what would happen when he opened the door and let down the ramp.

He need not have worried, for when he did so, Angelique emerged with one hop, threw herself about his neck once more and kissed him passionately. The action brought forth laughter and a cheer from the spectators.

Now this had an immediate effect upon the kangaroo. Crowds, laughter and applause to her meant performance. So she began looking to Monsieur Durand, her new friend, for cues. He suddenly found himself in the extraordinary position of Mr Flippo.

Hardly knowing what had come over him, but remembering what he had seen on the television that night, he took Jean-Pierre from Cecile and popped him into Angelique's pouch. The Guinea Pig immediately disappeared. Monsieur Durand, in not too bad an imitation of Mr Flippo, pretended to look for him.

Jean-Pierre had been trained to remain hidden while he was being searched for. But as soon as the back was turned upon him, he would pop out his head from the pouch. This always brought gratifying shrieks of delight from the audience.

Monsieur Durand had not Angelique's props to hand and he certainly had no intention of boxing with her. So instead of her ball, he gave her his hat to balance on the end of her nose. This she did with great success. There were cries of 'Bravo!' in which Cecile joined delightedly. Angelique took a bow and Monsieur Durand did likewise. It was only at that instant that he saw his wife looking at him from the edge of the crowd and for a moment felt a little sheepish.

Later, down in the cellar where she had gone to feed her pet in the accustomed place beneath the arch, Cecile thought: *Why, Papa was doing just what I wanted to do. He was playing circus. It isn't fair!*

But then she knew that things that were not fair were part of the life of every child. Angelique and the caravan were hers. They had been given to her. Not only had her father been amusing himself with them, but she was not to be allowed to keep them.

It was indeed true what Cecile had guessed. Monsieur Durand *had* been 'playing circus'. And now that the neighbours had gone, he realized that he had been caught off his guard by a memory of his own boyhood. Once, when a travelling show had passed by, he had longed desperately to run off with it. There he had been today, tricked by this memory into making a spectacle of himself.

He went to find some rope to put around Angelique's neck, but it was unnecessary. The absurd creature was apparently quite mad about him. Wherever he went, she followed him to the great annoyance of Bobi, who barked jealously and hysterically. What to do?

He was aware of a struggle going on within himself. He looked around for Cecile, but she was nowhere to be seen. In the barn he made a bed of the straw used to cover his flowers in the winter and said to Angelique, giving her a pat, 'Just you stay there now, like a good girl.' She settled down at once contentedly. 'Who would have believed it?' Monsieur Durand said to himself.

His wife was already busying herself in the kitchen, so he went out and drove the caravan up the hill behind the house and parked it between two of his greenhouses. Then he returned and entering his study, consulted the encyclopaedia there, under the heading of 'Kangaroo'.

His finger moved down the page until he came to the part which caused him to shout, 'Ha! They're herbivorous,' which meant that they ate only vegetables and leafy things. Here he read, 'They will feed on berries, roots, fallen fruits, grass, leaves or vines. . . .'

Roots would include turnips and carrots, such as they grew in their garden. No doubt it would eat cabbage and certainly there were plenty of vines to be had after the grape harvest. Why, it was practically the diet of Cecile's Guinea Pig, Jean-Pierre.

And with that he shut the book and fell to thinking seriously about his daughter. He went over the affair beginning with the telephone call from Monsieur Bouglione in Paris. It seemed to him that never at any time since then had the circus been wholly out of his head, even when he had shouted at his wife, 'If someone willed one to us, would you expect me to take it out on the road?' He knew now that he would have liked nothing better.

What, then, more natural than that a child who had been left a trained kangaroo and a glamorous wagon, should be wildly excited and long to play with them?

He was still lost in his thoughts when Madame Durand appeared at the door of his study to enquire, 'Have you telephoned to the Prince yet?'

'Eh? What?' replied her husband. 'Prince? What prince?'

'Why Prince Rainier of course. About offering him the kangaroo.'

So much had happened since Monsieur Durand had had this idea of disposing of the unwelcome guest, that he had quite forgotten. The notion suddenly seemed no longer attractive. Shut Angelique away in a cage where she could not perform her tricks? Separate her from her friend the Guinea Pig to whom she had taken such a fancy? And no one to kiss? And here Monsieur Durand was thinking of the strange attachment the animal had formed for *him*. Why, she might pine away and die.

He said, 'There's no hurry. I want to reflect upon the matter a little. After all, she's a gentle creature and not doing anyone any harm. . . .'

His wife, wise like all wives, suspected she knew what was on her husband's mind. But she wished to be sure. And so she said, 'André Durand! Are you thinking of keeping that beast here? And after you have said you would not do so under any circumstances?'

As she had expected she succeeded in ruffling his feathers.

'Beast? Why she's adorable and . . .' But here he caught a twitch at the corner of his wife's mouth and a smile came to his own. 'Very well. You have caught me out. But since I have calmed down I have been thinking seriously. I was wrong. The animal actually belongs to Cecile. It was left to her in the will of that poor man she befriended. We have actually no right to dispose of it. We have a place in the barn where it seems quite contented. And see here . . .' and he pointed to the open pages of the encyclopaedia.

71

'She eats all the things we grow for ourselves. She wouldn't be any expense.'

'And the caravan,' Madame Durand asked mischievously, 'the one you said you wouldn't be found dead in?'

They both glanced out of the rear window of Monsieur Durand's study. From there they could see the rows of greenhouses on the hillside above. The gaudy circus wagon was standing between two of them. The midday sun shone upon the red and gold wagon with its merry blue lettering. And it penetrated the glass of the hot-houses to illuminate the matching colours of the flowers within.

'You know,' admitted André Durand, 'it looks rather good where it is. I mean it breaks up the line of all that glass. It takes the eye.'

At which they both threw their arms about one another and burst into roars of laughter.

The sound penetrated to Cecile in the cellar. She wondered what the joke was. Something grown-up no doubt. At least she had Jean-Pierre. She hugged him to her.

'How happy Cecile will be,' said her mother. 'She had her heart set on having them. You must go and tell her at once.'

'Yes, but wait,' he replied. 'Come with me.'

Together they went outside to the caravan. They both climbed in. Monsieur Durand started the engine and drove it round to the front of the house. The entrance to the cellar steps was there. Then Monsieur Durand went to the barn and fetched Angelique.

'Cecile,' her father called down to her.

'Yes, Papa!'

'It's dark down there in the cellar. Come up into the sunshine.'

'Yes, Papa.' Cecile wondered what was wanted now. Picking up Jean-Pierre she climbed the stairs, came out and stood there blinking in the bright light. Then she saw Angelique, the circus wagon and her mother and father.

'Oh,' she cried, 'they're going! You're taking them away!'

It was Monsieur Durand who gathered his daughter into his arms and said, 'No, Cecile. We are not. They are yours to keep. They may remain here as long as you want them.'

Angelique came over and kissed them both. It was a day that Cecile was to remember as long as she lived.